JESS & JAYLEN

VIDEO GAME ZOMBIE

BY BLAKE HOENA • ILLUSTRATED BY DANA REGAN

Published by The Child's World®
1980 Lookout Drive • Mankato, MN 56003-1705
800-599-READ • www.childsworld.com

Acknowledgments
The Child's World®: Mary Berendes, Publishing Director
The Design Lab: Design
Red Line Editorial: Editorial direction and production

ISBN 9781631434433
LCCN 2014930640

Printed in the United States of America
Mankato, MN
July, 2014
PA02215

TABLE OF CONTENTS

CHAPTER ONE

BIRTHDAY PARTY

"HAPPY BIRTHDAY TO YOU!" Jaylen's friends screamed at the tops of their lungs.

In front of him sat a birthday cake. Not only did it look like a robot but it also had glowing eyes. Instead of candles, nine white LED lights blinked on its chest.

"YOU LIVE IN A ZOO!" his friends continued singing.

Behind Jaylen's friends stood his older brother, Jack. Jack held up their little sister, Jenny, so she could see the cake. It was her idea to sing the "monkey" version of the happy birthday song. She giggled as she sang.

"YOU LOOK LIKE A MONKEY!"

Next to Jack and Jenny stood their parents. Jaylen's mom had made the cake. She modeled it after a robot from his favorite video game, *Ragin' Robots.*

"YOU SMELL LIKE ONE TOO!" everyone shouted.

Jaylen and his friends scarfed down the cake and ice cream. Then it was time for gifts. First, Jaylen's mom made him open the cards from his grandparents and aunts and uncles. But she wouldn't let him just rip them open and dump the money they held on the table. No. That would be too easy. He had to read each card out loud and say who it was from.

It was painful. One card said "You Rock" and had a picture of a cat banging on drums. Another showed a monkey wearing a birthday hat and read, "It's your birthday. Go bananas!"

Maybe that was funny a hundred years ago, Jaylen thought.

He rolled his eyes with each bad joke. His friends groaned and laughed with him.

Next up were the presents from his friends. This was his favorite part of the party. His friends knew what he really liked. They wouldn't give him something he "needed." No superhero underwear or sweaters. That's the type of stuff his mom always gave him. Jaylen's friends got him stuff he wanted. Toys. Games. Action figures. Fun stuff.

Jaylen saved Jess's gift for last. She lived just down the block from him. They had been best friends practically forever. She knew what he liked more than anyone.

Jess's present was huge. It took up half the table.

Jaylen tore off the wrapping paper. Under that was a cardboard box. Tucked inside the large box was a medium-sized box. It was sealed in a thick layer of duct tape.

"Aw, come on," Jaylen groaned. He lifted up the duct-taped box for everyone to see.

His friends snickered, and his little sister giggled. His mother snapped photos to post online.

Jaylen needed help from his dad to cut through the duct tape.

He couldn't believe it. That box was stuffed with small foam packing peanuts!

Jaylen glared at Jess. She just smiled back at him. He dug through the packing peanuts and found a small box covered in wrapping paper. It was about the size of a video game case.

Cool, he thought. *Jess got me something good.*

Jaylen ripped through the wrapping paper, tore open the box, and inside he found . . . socks.

What? Jaylen thought, confused.

The socks were gray with superheroes on them. His sister giggled while his mom snapped pictures.

"You left those at my house last week after skateboarding," Jess said. "I thought you'd want them back."

Jaylen didn't know what to say.

"They were stinking up the place," Jess added. "So my mom washed them."

"Um, thanks," Jaylen said.

He looked around at his friends. His brother and sister. He wasn't sure, but he thought something was up. Everyone was starting to chuckle.

"What?" Jaylen said. "What's so funny?"

"Bro, the look on your face," Jack said. "You look like you're about to cry."

"Am not," Jaylen shot back.

Jess walked over to him. He could tell she was trying hard not to laugh.

"Relax, that's not your present," Jess said. "I just had to mess with you, after what you did on *my* birthday."

At Jess's party, Jaylen had switched the candles on her cake with relighting ones. She tried to blow them out. But they just kept sparking back up. She was breathing so hard after a few tries that Jaylen had worried she would pass out.

Jess pulled out a video game box from under the table. It was *Zombie Attack*.

"No way!" Jaylen said excitedly. He snatched the game from Jess. "I've been trying to find this forever."

"I know," Jess said, grinning. "I've watched you dig through every used game bin in the city."

Zombie Attack was a classic. Jaylen had played *Zombie Attack II: Save Your Brains* and *Zombie Attack III: Who Needs Brains?* But never the original game in the series. The game that started it all. This was the best gift ever.

"Where'd you find it?" he asked.

"I was visiting my dad in the 'burbs," Jess said. "He took me to a used game exchange."

"Cool!"

Suddenly, Jaylen wished the party was over. He wanted to play his new game and rid the world of brain-eating zombies.

CHAPTER TWO

MONDAY MORNING

Jess was late for the school bus as usual. She had just stepped outside her apartment when she saw it starting to pull away.

Nuts! she thought.

Luckily, Jaylen was on that bus. He was never late, and he was always watching for her. She was sure he would let Mr. Yaseen, the bus driver, know she was making a dash for it. Then the bus would stop and wait for her.

Jess took off after the bus. She yelled, "Wait! Wait!" and waved her arms. People jumped out of the way.

But today, the bus didn't stop. It just sped away.

Jess thought she saw Jaylen near the front of the bus. He was staring out the window with a blank look on his face.

Kind of like a zombie, she thought.

Now Jess needed to ride the city bus to school. That would take an extra 15 minutes because she had to switch buses near Washington Park. Jess let her mom know and headed to the bus stop.

By the time Jess finally arrived at Emerson Elementary, she was steaming mad. Her best friend had ditched her. And she didn't have any time to hang out with her friends before class.

She plopped down in her in seat next to Jaylen just before the final bell rang. When he said hello, she replied with a "Hmpf!"

"You missed the bus," he said.

"Yeah, no thanks to you," she shot back.

"What'd I do?" he asked.

"You didn't have Mr. Yaseen stop the bus for me," she replied.

"What? Really?" he said. "I never even saw you."

Jess knew her best friend wouldn't lie to her. But she couldn't believe he hadn't seen her. She'd been waving her arms like a wild animal!

"I was tired this morning," Jaylen went on. "I'm surprised I made it on time. I must have spaced out on the bus."

By lunch, Jess had forgiven Jaylen. She also found out why he was so tired. They were sitting with their friends Tanya and Tou. Jaylen started talking about *Zombie Attack*.

"There's this zombie horde on level two," he said, nearly jumping out of his seat. "I stayed up all night defeating it."

Jess listened patiently. She knew her friend. When he got excited about something new, he couldn't let it go. The same thing had happened when they'd decided to enter a skateboarding contest. Jaylen had spent

all his time looking at online videos of tricks
he could try.

But by the bus ride home that afternoon,
Jess was getting sick of hearing about
zombies. Jaylen didn't seem to notice.

"I hope I get past level three tonight!" he
said as he waved good-bye.

CHAPTER THREE

NOT AGAIN!

Tuesday began the same way Monday had.

Nuts! Jess thought as she watched the school bus speed away.

Once again, she would have to take the city bus. She turned to go back to her apartment. She needed to tell her mom.

As she spun around, she saw Jaylen standing on the sidewalk behind her. His jaw hung open as he watched the bus drive away.

"Whoa!" Jess said. "OK, who are you, and what have you done with Jaylen?"

"Huh?" Jaylen said.

He looked sleepy and confused.

"Just messing with you," Jess said. But he wasn't getting it. She tried again.

"You missed the bus. You never miss the bus."

"That is not good," he said.

Jaylen sounded out of it, like his brains were scrambled. He looked out of it, too. His face was pale, and he had a blank look.

He's been zombified, Jess thought.

"It's not a big deal," she said. "We can ride the city bus to school. I do it all the time."

They let their folks know what had happened. Jess's mom wasn't surprised that her daughter had missed the bus again. But Jaylen's dad was not happy.

"Did you forget to set your alarm clock?" he asked.

"No. I was just waiting for Jess and forgot to check the time," Jaylen lied.

He didn't want to admit that he had stayed up late again playing *Zombie Attack*. If his dad knew that video games were an issue, Jaylen would lose his privilege to play them. Those were two words his dad liked to use a lot. *Issue* and *privilege*. Any time Jaylen did something wrong, like leave his room a mess, his dad said it was an issue. That led to a discussion about privileges. They discussed whether he had earned the privilege to hang out with his friends. Or play video games while his room was such a mess.

Talking to parents was difficult sometimes. Luckily, Jaylen's dad believed him this time.

On the bus, Jaylen told Jess the truth.

"There's this lake filled with zombie fish," he explained. "I couldn't figure out how to cross it. So I stayed up late."

Jaylen went on and on about the game. Jess rolled her eyes.

More zombies… great, she thought.

Jaylen didn't stop talking about zombies until they got to school and the bell rang.

Then at lunch, he started up again.

"Enough, already!" Tanya groaned. "Who bought you that stupid game anyway?"

Jess looked down at her lunch tray. She was starting to wish she hadn't gone through all the trouble of finding the game.

"Next time, all you're getting is socks," she warned Jaylen.

But that didn't stop him from talking about *Zombie Attack.* On the bus ride home, Jess had to listen to Jaylen talk about a zombie zoo in the video game. Apparently there were zombie lions and zombie elephants that chased you.

"So, wanna hang out tonight?" Jess
asked once they got off the bus.

"Nah, I gotta kill zombies," Jaylen said.

Jess felt her stomach sink as she watched
Jaylen walk toward his apartment building.

Her best friend was choosing a video
game over her!

CHAPTER FOUR

POP QUIZ

Wednesday morning was not much different than Tuesday morning. Only this time, Jaylen's dad asked a few more questions about why he had missed the bus.

"Are you feeling OK?" he asked. "Did you get to bed too late last night? You aren't staying up late playing video games, are you? Are you sure your alarm clock is working?"

"Yes! No! No! Yes!" Jaylen replied, hoping he'd given his replies in the right order. His dad liked to confuse Jaylen and his siblings by asking several yes-or-no questions at the same time. If they answered wrong, he knew he'd caught them in a lie.

Jaylen's dad let him go without much
of a fuss, so he must have gotten the
answers right.

During their math section that day, Mrs. Johnson told the class she had a surprise for them. She was smiling, but that didn't mean it was a good surprise. Mrs. Johnson was always smiling. If you got a good grade, she'd smile and say, "Good job!" If you got a bad grade, she'd say, "Better luck next time." Always smiling. It drove Jess and Jaylen crazy. Jaylen often tried convincing Jess that Mrs. Johnson was a robot, programmed to smile no matter what.

Jaylen looked at Jess.

"Robots are better than zombies, at least," he whispered. "They have computer brains. You can reason with them. Zombies just want to eat your brains."

Jess rolled her eyes.

It was definitely not a good surprise.

"As you know, we've been studying the metric system," Mrs. Johnson smiled. "So today, we're going to have a pop quiz to see how well you understand it. You will be doing some metric conversions, so I will allow you to use calculators. You have ten minutes."

Mrs. Johnson handed out the quizzes.

Jess glanced at Jaylen. He was a math ace. Usually he started scribbling the answers the second he had a quiz on his desk. But something was wrong today. He was staring blankly at the quiz. He didn't even start writing until the time was almost up.

After school, Mrs. Johnson stopped Jaylen as he was about to go catch the bus. She held up his quiz. There was a big 4 on it. He had only gotten four out of 20 questions right.

"Jaylen," Mrs. Johnson began with a gentle smile. "If you're having trouble with the metric system, I can help you."

Jaylen gulped and shook his head. He had never bombed a test before. Just like he had never missed the bus before.

"Normally, when a student fails a test," Mrs. Johnson explained, still smiling, "I have them take it home to have their parents sign it. Since this is your first time, we don't have to do that. But you'll need to do better next time."

Jaylen nodded. Then he quickly ran to catch his bus. He would have hated explaining what had happened on the quiz to his dad. Failing a quiz would definitely be an issue. There would be privileges to discuss.

CHAPTER FIVE

ZOMBIE

Things didn't get any easier for Jaylen the rest of the week. He stayed up late playing his video game. He slept through his alarm. He missed the school bus. Then he rode to school on the city bus with Jess.

Not only was he looking pale, but his eyes were bloodshot, with dark circles under them. His clothes were wrinkled, and his hair was sticking up all over. On top of that, he was tired and cranky. So was Jess. But that was because whenever Jaylen opened his mouth, he was still talking about zombies.

"Dude, will you knock it off about zombies?" Tou said at lunch.

"Yeah, you're even beginning to look like one," Tanya added. "All pale and groaning."

"Zombies! Zooombies!" Tou and Tanya held out their arms in front of them and moaned. "Zooooombieeeeees!"

What Jaylen did next surprised them all. He stood up and grabbed his tray. Then he went and sat down at an empty table. By himself.

~~~~

Jaylen's mood didn't improve the rest of the day.

"Don't forget to meet me at the skate park tomorrow," Jess told Jaylen after they got off the bus Friday.

The skate park was in Washington Park. Jess and Jaylen tried to go every weekend. Saturday mornings were reserved for junior skateboarders like them.

Jaylen just walked away.

Fridays were usually Jaylen's night to chill. After a long school week, he liked to shut himself in his room and unwind. Usually by playing video games. He

still had a few levels left to conquer on
Zombie Attack.

After dinner, he grabbed a big glass of
juice and a box of crackers. He was planning
on pulling an all-nighter. He shut the door
to his room and turned on his game console.
Loud groaning and moaning noises filled the
room as zombies appeared on the TV screen.

Time to bash some zombies, Jaylen thought.

Lights flashed. People screamed.
Zombies called out for brains. Jaylen jerked
the joystick on his controller. He madly
thumbed buttons as he hacked and slashed
his way through the zombie hordes.

Jaylen wasn't sure how long he'd
been playing when he hit pause to take a
bathroom break. He opened his bedroom
door and walked down the hallway.
Everything was quiet and dark. The only

light was from a streetlight shining through the living room window.

What time is it? he wondered.

Moments later, he was back at it. Hacking at zombies. More screaming. More slashing.

He didn't stop until there was a knock on his door.

"Jaylen?" A voice called from the other side of the door.

"Yeah," Jaylen said. He didn't turn from his game.

"It's Jess," the voice said.

The door creaked open.

"What are you doing?" Jess asked.

"Ridding the world of zombies," Jaylen said, eyes still on the screen.

Jess leaned against the doorway and crossed her arms.

"You weren't at the skate park," she said. "What happened? I waited all morning."

Jaylen kept tapping the buttons on his controller. Screams and groans came from the TV screen.

Now Jess was getting mad. She was trying to talk to Jaylen. But he couldn't, or wouldn't, take his eyes off his TV screen. It was like he was in a zombie trance.

"Dude, seriously," she snapped after a few minutes. "Can you shut that off for a second?"

Jaylen still didn't look at her. So she walked over and hit the *OFF* button. The TV screen went black.

"Ahh!" Jaylen screamed. "Why'd you do that?"

Now he was mad, too.

"I spent all night working on that level," he cried.

"That's ALL you've been doing," Jess shouted back. "All week! Nothing but zombie this and zombie that."

Jess stood up and walked toward the door.

"Saturdays at the skate park are supposed to be our thing," Jess said. "And you totally blew me off!"

Just then, Jaylen's dad poked his head into the room.

"Is there an issue in here?" he asked. "I heard shouting."

"No, Dad," Jaylen said, glaring at Jess. "It was just a problem with my game."

His dad looked over at the black screen.

"Well, your mom worked the night shift last night, so keep it down," he said. "Or we'll have to discuss your video game privileges."

Jaylen's dad made a face as he turned to walk away. "Something smells funny in here," he added.

"Great," Jaylen said to Jess, after his dad had left. "Thanks for getting me in trouble."

"What, you're blaming me?" Jess said. "It's not my fault that you've been missing the bus and failing tests! And by the way, that funny smell," she added, "is *you*!"

She stomped out of Jaylen's room and headed home.

Jaylen turned back to the TV screen. He leaned over to turn his console on. He could continue from his last save. It might take him all day. But he could finish the level.

In the still-black screen, Jaylen could see his reflection. His hair was a mess. He looked down at his clothes. There was a juice stain on his shirt. Cracker crumbs covered his lap. And there was that funny smell.

Jess is right, he thought. *It's me! I stink!*

He couldn't remember the last time he had taken a shower. At least since he started playing *Zombie Attack*.

Oh no! Jaylen suddenly became frightened. *I am turning into a zombie!*

CHAPTER SIX

MONDAY MORNING, AGAIN

Monday morning, Jaylen was early to the bus stop.

The bus screeched to a halt at the corner. The doors *whooshed* open. Jaylen greeted Mr. Yaseen before taking a seat near the front of the bus.

Then he peeked out his window and watched for Jess.

Sure enough, just as the bus lurched forward, she popped outside.

"Mr. Yaseen, wait, it's Jess," Jaylen said.

Mr. Yaseen rolled his eyes. But he waited.

A busload of kids turned to watch Jess run for the bus.

People leaped out of her way as she yelled, "Wait! Wait!" and waved her arms wildly. Today, she had a half-eaten granola bar sticking out of her mouth. Her jacket was unzipped, and a comb was caught in her hair.

Jess leaped onto the bus. Jaylen scooted over so she could sit next to him. But she looked around for another seat.

"Jess, come on," he said as she was about to walk past him.

She glared at him. She was still mad.

"I took a shower. Smell!" Jaylen said, lifting his arm to show her his armpit.

The corners of her lips curled up.

"Not in a million years," she said as she plopped down next to him. They sat in silence for a few moments.

"I'm sorry about Saturday," Jaylen said.

"Hmpf," was her reply.

"You were right, you know," he said.

Jess didn't say anything. She just sat with her arms crossed.

"It was my fault," he went on. "Missing the bus. Messing up on that quiz."

They were quiet for a moment as the bus rumbled down the street.

"After you left Saturday," he said, "well, after I took a shower, I mean— my dad didn't want to talk to me until I cleaned up—I told him I had an issue with video games."

"Really?" Jess said. She was still trying to act annoyed. She faced forward in her seat. But she watched him out of the corner of her eye.

"Yeah," he continued. "I told him the real reason I missed the bus. And about that quiz."

Jess turned to him, wide-eyed.

"No way!" she said. "Did he take your game system away?"

"Nope," Jaylen said. "He said I earned the privilege to keep it because I was trying to be responsible."

Responsibility was another word Jaylen's dad liked to say a lot. Even more than "issue" or "privilege."

"But he did suggest I limit my game time," Jaylen added. "So I might be done with zombies for a while."

"Does that mean you don't want to be zombies for Halloween anymore?" Jess asked. "Because I think we could make the creepiest costumes."

"No way!" Jaylen said excitedly. "That'd be so cool."

"Well, I'd need work on my costume," Jess said. "But I see you already have yours on."

"What?" Jaylen said, panicked. He looked down, expecting to see juice stains on his shirt and cracker crumbs all over his pants. "I showered, I swear!"

Jess smirked. She was just messing
with him.

"Not funny!" Jaylen said, laughing.

NOW IT'S YOUR TURN!

1. In the story, Jaylen mentions some words that his dad likes to use a lot: *issue*, *privilege*, and *responsibility*. Write a few sentences discussing what these words mean to you. How are these words related?

2. Jaylen gets easily caught up in video games. Is there an activity that you really enjoy, such as a hobby or a sport? Write down what it is, and explain what you like about this activity.

3. Who do you feel is the story's main character? Jess or Jaylen? Use examples from the story to explain your answer.

4. Jess and Jaylen are best friends, but even best friends can have disagreements. Have you ever argued with a friend? Write about it. What were you arguing about, and how was the disagreement settled?

5. Imagine that you are Jess. How would you react if you knew Jaylen was spending too much time playing video games? Would you be worried or upset? Would you forgive Jaylen or stop being his friend?

6. Jess and Jaylen like to tease and play pranks on each other. Have you ever played a joke on someone? Write about it. What did you do, and what happened? Was the person you played the joke on mad? Or did he or she laugh?

ABOUT THE AUTHOR

Blake Hoena grew up in central Wisconsin. In his youth, he wrote stories about robots conquering the moon and trolls lumbering around the woods behind his parents' house. Later, he moved to Minnesota to pursue a master of fine arts degree in creative writing from Minnesota State University, Mankato. He now lives in Saint Paul with his wife, two kids, a dog, and a couple of cats.

Blake has written more than 60 books for children—everything from ABC books about dogs to a series of graphic novels about two alien brothers bent on conquering Earth, chapter books about Batman and Superman, and retellings of classic stories such as *Treasure Island* and *Peter Pan*.

ABOUT THE ILLUSTRATOR

Dana Regan is originally from Lake Nebagamon, Wisconsin, and has her bachelor of fine arts degree in illustration from Washington University in Saint Louis, Missouri. She has illustrated more than 75 books and written seven early reader books, which, collectively, have sold more than 1 million copies. She lives and works in Kansas City, Missouri, with her sons, Joe and Tommy, who are a constant source of inspiration and tech support.